HORNBEAM
GETS
IT
DONE

Cynthia Rylant • Arthur Howard

Beach Lane Books   New York   London   Toronto   Sydney   New Delhi

BEACH LANE BOOKS
An imprint of Simon & Schuster Children's Publishing Division
1230 Avenue of the Americas, New York, New York 10020
Text © 2024 by Cynthia Rylant
Illustration © 2024 by Arthur Howard
Book design by Irene Metaxatos © 2024 by Simon & Schuster, LLC
BEACH LANE BOOKS and colophon are trademarks of Simon & Schuster, LLC.
Simon & Schuster: Celebrating 100 Years of Publishing in 2024
For information about special discounts for bulk purchases, please contact Simon & Schuster Special Sales at 1-866-506-1949
or business@simonandschuster.com.
The Simon & Schuster Speakers Bureau can bring authors to your live event. For more information or to book an event,
contact the Simon & Schuster Speakers Bureau at 1-866-248-3049 or visit our website at www.simonspeakers.com.
The text for this book was set in Griffo Classico.
The illustrations for this book were rendered in colored pencil, watercolor, and gouache on Stonehenge paper.
Manufactured in China
0124 SCP
First Edition
2 4 6 8 10 9 7 5 3 1
Library of Congress Cataloging-in-Publication Data
Names: Rylant, Cynthia, author. | Howard, Arthur, illustrator.
Title: Hornbeam gets it done / Cynthia Rylan ; illustrated by Arthur Howard.
Description: First edition. | New York : Beach Lane Books, 2024. | Series: The Hornbeam books | Audience: Ages 4-8. |
Audience: Grades 2-3. | Summary: Hornbeam the moose saves his blueberry bush from blowing away with the help of his
friend Eureka, goes grocery shopping with Cuddy, and enjoys game night with Eureka, Cuddy, and Adorabelle.
Identifiers: LCCN 2023032043 (print) | LCCN 2023032044 (ebook) | ISBN 9781665924832 (hardcover) |
ISBN 9781665924849 (ebook)
Subjects: CYAC: Moose—Fiction. | Animals—Fiction. | Friendship—Fiction. | LCGFT: Animal fiction.
Classification: LCC PZ7.R982 Ht 2024 (print) | LCC PZ7.R982 (ebook) | DDC [E]—dc23
LC record available at https://lccn.loc.gov/2023032043
LC ebook record available at https://lccn.loc.gov/2023032044

Contents

March Worries

Every March the wind picked up at Hornbeam's house. Hornbeam could hear it coming. *Whoosh!* The windows rattled. The wind chimes chimed. The weather vane went round and round.

March days were windy days!

But this March, Hornbeam was worried about the wind. He had planted a little blueberry bush. Hornbeam was worried that the wind would blow it away. He could see all the blueberry muffins and blueberry pies blowing away with his blueberry bush.

He decided to protect it.

Hornbeam got an umbrella and stood beside the blueberry bush. But the wind came along—*whoosh!*—and turned the umbrella inside out.

Hornbeam would just have to tie the bush to something sturdy. Eureka's house was right there. It was sturdy. He would tie the blueberry bush to that.

Hornbeam found a lot of rope. He tied one end around the bush. Then Hornbeam walked all around Eureka's house. He climbed onto the roof. He cut across the porch.

Hornbeam was still looking for just the right spot to tie the other end of his rope when Eureka stepped outside.

"Hornbeam!" Eureka said. "Why is my house all tied up?"

Hornbeam stepped back and looked at Eureka's house, awash with rope.

"I was trying to keep my blueberry bush from blowing away," said Hornbeam.

"Well, just use a garden stake," said Eureka.

Eureka's shed was full of garden stakes. He tied Hornbeam's bush to one of them.

Whoosh went the wind. The little bush did not budge.

"Thank you," said Hornbeam. "I can unrope your house now."

"I'll help," said Eureka.

As they were unroping Eureka's house, Hornbeam saw his pine tree and his rosebush and his bird feeder and many other things struggling in the wind.

It was a good thing that Hornbeam had so much rope and Eureka had so many stakes!
All through March the wind went *whoosh!*

But not one thing budged in Hornbeam's yard.

Food-Shopping

Hornbeam and Cuddy liked to food-shop together every Monday. There were not many shoppers on Mondays. So they could pick and choose in peace and quiet.

But there was always one problem.

The problem was that the baked goods were right inside the front door. When Hornbeam and Cuddy rolled in their carts, the cupcakes were staring right at them.

There is not a moose or a bull anywhere who does not love a cupcake. So Hornbeam and Cuddy did not get very far after they walked into the store every Monday.

They each bought a cupcake. They each got a juice. And the newspaper.

They spread everything out on a market table. And they sat there for about two hours. Eating cupcakes. Drinking juice. Reading the paper. But not food-shopping.

When they were finally ready to food-shop, they were both too full and too lazy to care. So they did not do a very good job. Maybe an apple. A jar of peanut butter. They were way too full to think about bread.

They went home with very small bags.

Hornbeam and Cuddy did this every Monday. And then they had to go back to the market on Tuesday because they were out of food!

Hornbeam and Cuddy knew that they must not look at the cupcakes on Tuesdays, or they would have to come back to the market again on Wednesdays!

So on Tuesdays they always wore blinders. Hornbeam and Cuddy walked all around the store, and they were very good food-shoppers.

One Tuesday a very pink shopper asked Hornbeam why he was wearing blinders. Hornbeam confessed that he wore blinders so that he would not eat cupcakes.

"You mean the ones by the front door?" the shopper asked.

"Yes," said Hornbeam.

"Oh, I have that problem too," the shopper said. "I have to put a hot pepper in my mouth so that I will not want a cupcake and I can get my food-shopping done."

"Really?" asked Hornbeam.

"Hot peppers will get the job done," said the shopper.

So every Tuesday after that, Hornbeam and Cuddy walked into the market to food-shop with hot peppers in their mouths. And they got it done!

Of course, they both knew that if they used hot peppers on *Mondays*, they could save themselves a trip.

But neither said anything about that.

Game Night

Once a month Eureka hosted Game Night at his house.

Hornbeam, Cuddy, and Adorabelle all arrived carrying snacks. Hornbeam brought the chips.

Cuddy brought the ginger ale. And Adorabelle brought the chocolate-covered raisins.

Eureka had a big, round table that was perfect for games.
And he always wore a hat that said "Game On."

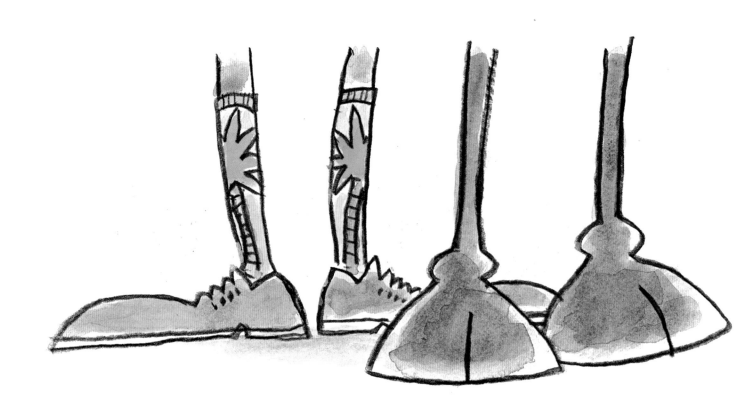

Hornbeam always wore his tropical socks. Adorabelle always wore her lucky watch.

And Cuddy always wore his mirror sunglasses.

Hornbeam did not like Cuddy's mirror sunglasses. When he looked at Cuddy, Hornbeam saw himself in the mirror. Then he started worrying about the size of his nose or if he needed a haircut.

So he looked at Cuddy sideways instead.

Eureka had a lot of board games. There was Cookie Town and Mystery Mansion. There was Trouble and Trapped!

But the group favorite was Dream Trip. Everyone loved
Dream Trip. Each player got to travel to an unusual place
on the game board. This was exciting. And the player who
traveled the most miles at the end of the game was the winner.

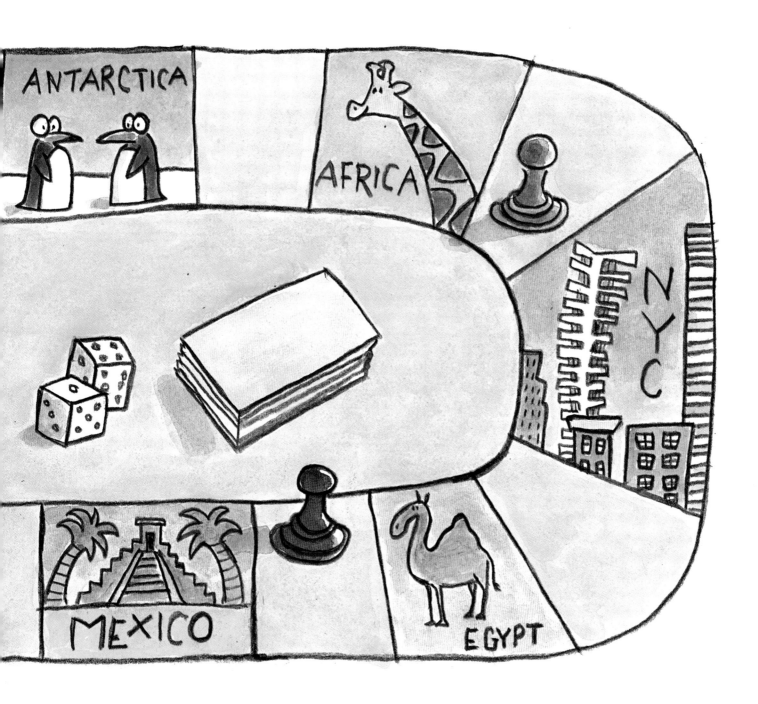

Sometimes Eureka won, with his "Game On" hat.

Sometimes Hornbeam won,
with his tropical socks.

Sometimes Adorabelle won, with her lucky watch.

And sometimes Cuddy won. When he did, he took off his mirror sunglasses.

"Cuddy!" said Hornbeam happily. "I see you and not me!"

Whoever won the game had to bring a surprise to the next game night.

Hornbeam once brought his baby pictures. Adorabelle once brought her seashell collection.

Cuddy once brought a movie camera.

And if Eureka won, everyone got to poke around in his attic.

Game Night was always a fun night for all.
And no matter who won, everybody went home happy!